A REWARD FOR JOSEFINA

JOSEFINA · 1824

BY VALERIE TRIPP

ILLUSTRATIONS JEAN-PAUL TIBBLES

VIGNETTES SUSAN MCALILEY

THE AMERICAN GIRLS COLLECTION®

Published by Pleasant Company Publications
© Copyright 1999 by Pleasant Company
For information, address: Book Editor, Pleasant Company Publications,
8400 Fairway Place, P.O. Box 620998, Middleton, WI 53562.

Printed in Hong Kong.
99 00 01 02 03 04 05 06 C&C 10 9 8 7 6 5

The American Girls Collection®, Josefina®, and Josefina Montoya®
are trademarks of Pleasant Company.

Edited by Nancy Holyoke and Michelle Jones
Art Directed and Designed by Tricia Doherty and Laura Moberly

Library of Congress Cataloging-in-Publication Data

Tripp, Valerie, 1951-
A reward for Josefina / by Valerie Tripp;
illustrations, Jean-Paul Tibbles; vignettes, Susan McAliley.
p. cm. — (The American girls collection)
Summary: When the entire family goes into the hills to collect
piñon nuts, Josefina hopes to find the most in order to make
Tía Dolores proud of her.

ISBN 1-56247-763-3
[1. Pine nuts—Fiction. 2. Aunts—Fiction.
3. Ranch life—New Mexico—Fiction. 4. Mexican Americans—Fiction.
5. New Mexico—History—To 1848—Fiction.]
I. Tibbles, Jean-Paul, ill. II. McAliley, Susan. III. Title. IV. Series.
PZ7.T7363Re 1999 [Fic]—dc21 98-42856 CIP AC

The
AMERICAN GIRLS
COLLECTION
™

OTHER AMERICAN GIRLS
SHORT STORIES:

FELICITY'S NEW SISTER

KIRSTEN ON THE TRAIL

HIGH HOPES FOR ADDY

SAMANTHA'S WINTER PARTY

MOLLY TAKES FLIGHT

PICTURE CREDITS

The following organizations have generously given permission to reprint illustrations contained in "Looking Back": p. 32—La Hacienda de los Martínez, Taos, New Mexico; p. 33—School of American Research Collections, Museum of New Mexico, photo by Ben Wittick, #15754; p. 34—Museum of New Mexico, #49167, photo by William H. Jackson; p. 35—New Mexico State Records Center and Archives; p. 36—Photo by SCS, Selgem #87.45.493, courtesy Maxwell Museum of Anthropology, University of New Mexico, Albuquerque (bottom); p. 37—Corbis Bettman (horno); courtesy Montadori (corn); p. 38—Edward S. Curtis, Library of Congress; p. 40—Photography by Jamie Young.

TABLE OF CONTENTS

PAPÁ
Josefina's father, who guides his family and his rancho with quiet strength.

ANA
Josefina's oldest sister, who is married and has two little boys.

JOSEFINA
A nine-year-old girl whose heart and hopes are as big as the New Mexico sky.

FRANCISCA
Josefina's fifteen-year-old sister, who is headstrong and impatient.

CLARA
Josefina's practical, sensible sister, who is twelve years old.

TÍA DOLORES
*Josefina's aunt, who
has lived far away in
Mexico City for ten years.*

ANTONIO
AND JUAN
*Ana's little boys,
who are one and
three years old.*

Josefina and her family speak Spanish, so you'll see some Spanish words in this book. If you can't tell what a word means from reading the story or looking at the illustrations, you can turn to the "Glossary of Spanish Words" that begins on page 48. It will tell you what the word means and how to pronounce it.

Remember that in Spanish, "j" is pronounced like "h." That means Josefina's name is pronounced "ho-seh-FEE-nah."

A REWARD FOR JOSEFINA

Josefina walked quickly and skipped every few steps to match Tía Dolores's long strides. It was just before dawn on a cold, clear day. Josefina and Tía Dolores were walking up into the foothills of the mountains to gather *piñón* nuts. Papá was ahead of them, and Josefina could hear her sisters behind her, huffing and puffing as the path grew steeper.

Josefina liked the energetic way

Tía Dolores walked. In fact, she liked everything about her young aunt—from her wholehearted way of laughing to her strong, square hands to the way Tía Dolores listened, *really* listened, when Josefina spoke. Tía Dolores had recently come to live on Papá's *rancho*. Josefina and her sisters wanted Tía Dolores to be happy there, and so each sister tried hard in her own way to please her.

"Look," said Josefina, pointing. "The sun's coming up over the mountain."

"Ah!" said Tía Dolores. She smiled, first at the sun and then at Josefina. "God has given us a fine day."

"*Sí,*" said Clara, Josefina's next oldest sister. "A fine day for our hard work."

"Look," said Josefina, pointing. "The sun's coming up over the mountain."

"Oh, Clara," laughed Josefina. "Gathering piñón nuts isn't *work*. It's fun."

But Clara wanted Tía Dolores to know how practical she was. "It's important that we gather a good harvest of piñón nuts," she said seriously. "Papá trades them for things we need. They're valuable."

"They're delicious!" said Francisca, Josefina's second oldest sister, who never worried about being practical. Francisca ran ahead, then turned around and walked backward so that she was facing Tía Dolores. "On winter evenings," she said, "we sit by the fire and roast the nuts and crack them and eat them, one after another! Oh, it makes me hungry just to *think* of it!"

"Don't get hungry yet," warned Ana. "Lunchtime is hours away." Ana was the oldest sister. She had helped Carmen, the cook, pack a lunch for everyone to enjoy at noon. It was carefully wrapped in a sack that was tied to the mule Carmen's husband Miguel was leading. Ana's little boy Juan was on the mule, too. Juan was only three, and his legs were so short they stuck straight out on either side of the mule's back. Ana carried her baby, Antonio, on her hip. He was only one year old and too little to ride the mule.

Tía Dolores lifted Antonio out of

Ana's arms. "Let me carry this stout fellow," she said.

"*Gracias*," said Ana. She and Tía Dolores exchanged a smile.

When Josefina saw that smile she felt a terrible pang of jealousy. She knew she shouldn't envy Ana the special affection and respect that Tía Dolores had for her. After all, Tía Dolores and Ana were close in age. It made sense that they were more like friends than aunt and niece. And sweet, gentle Ana deserved Tía Dolores's respect. Hadn't she taken over the responsibility of running the household since Mamá's death over a year ago? But Josefina couldn't help envying Ana. Tía Dolores was always kind and loving to

Josefina, of course. But with all her heart,
Josefina wanted Tía Dolores to smile at
her the way she smiled at Ana—with
pride. She longed for Tía Dolores to think
of her as someone special.

Francisca had moved ahead of the
rest of them along the path. She called
back now, "Hurry up! Papá's waiting for
us." The sun caught the frost on the pine
trees and made it sparkle. Francisca had
thrown back her *rebozo*, and Josefina
could see sparkles in her hair, too,
where frost had fallen on it. Josefina
sighed. Francisca was just naturally
special. She could always make
Tía Dolores laugh because she was
so quick and lively. And Clara had already

rebozo

7

won Tía Dolores's praise for being careful with her sewing and weaving.

Maybe today will be my chance to impress Tía Dolores, thought Josefina. *Maybe I could save her from twisting her ankle, or falling off a cliff, or being eaten by a mountain lion!* Then Josefina laughed at herself. She knew perfectly well that Tía Dolores was the most surefooted of them all. And if a mountain lion should happen to bump into Tía Dolores, Josefina could easily picture her aunt shooing it away all on her own.

Papá was waiting for them in a clearing surrounded by scrub oaks,

cottonwoods, and a few piñón trees.
"This is a good place to build our fire,"
he said. "We'll spread out from here to
gather nuts from the trees on the hillside,
then we'll meet back here for lunch at
noon." His eyes twinkled as he spoke to
the sisters and Tía Dolores. "You'll have
to earn your lunch today. It will be your
reward for a sack full of piñón nuts. And
this year, I'm offering a special reward to
the one who gathers the most nuts. We'll
see whose sack is biggest at noontime."

All the sisters smiled. Josefina was so
happy she wanted to cheer out loud. At
last! Here was her chance to shine! She
was determined that no one would
collect more piñón nuts than she would.

Papá's reward—and Tía Dolores's admiration—would be hers.

Josefina picked up an empty sack. Her hopes were high, and she was eager to begin gathering. But Papá's next words sent her hopes crashing down. "Josefina, my little one," he said. "You stay here and help Carmen and Miguel. Keep the fire going, and keep an eye on Antonio and Juan."

"But *I* want to go, too!" wailed Juan. "I want to collect nuts and win the reward!" Josefina was glad. Juan had said aloud exactly what she was thinking!

Papá knelt next to Juan. "You and Josefina have a different job to do," he

said. "We'll be hungry when we return
from gathering nuts. We'll be very dis-
appointed if animals have stolen our
lunch away! You must guard it for us."
Papá smiled up at Josefina, saying,
"That's a very important job, isn't it,
Josefina?"

"Sí, Papá," said Josefina. Papá's

smile was warm, and Josefina tried hard
to return it as she handed her sack back
to him. But she was brokenhearted!
*I've just lost my best chance to impress
Tía Dolores*, she thought. *How can I collect
any nuts left behind here with the lunch and
the babies?*

Sadly, Josefina watched Papá and
Tía Dolores and her sisters walk away.
Their laughter and happy chatter faded
as they disappeared among the trees,
and soon it was quiet in the clearing.
Carmen spread a blanket on the ground,
and Juan and Antonio fell asleep on it.

Josefina helped Miguel start a fire,
and then Carmen asked her to stir a pot
of chile stew as it simmered. Josefina

was grumpy. *I might just as well have stayed home!* she thought. When Miguel said he was going to lead the mule to the stream, Josefina jumped up.

"May I go, too?" she asked eagerly. Anything was better than stirring stew and roasting herself by the fire like a *chile*!

"Sí . . ." Carmen began to say.

But in her eagerness Josefina had spoken too loudly and awakened Antonio. The baby began fussing and crying so much that he woke Juan, too.

Carmen rocked Antonio in her arms, but his wails only grew louder. "Antonio is hungry," she said. "I'll have to take him to Ana so that she can nurse him."

Carmen looked at Josefina. "You must stay here and look after Juan. And keep an eye on the lunch."

"I will," sighed Josefina, sinking down next to the fire again.

As soon as Miguel and Carmen left, Juan spoke up. "I want lunch now," he said. "I'm hungry."

Josefina couldn't help grinning. "You're always hungry," she said. "We can't have lunch until everyone comes back from picking nuts."

"I want to pick nuts, too!" said Juan.

"We don't have a sack," Josefina answered.

Juan pointed to the sack the lunch was packed in. "I want *this* sack," he said. He started to untie it.

Josefina could see that she had better find something for Juan to do, or he'd never stop pestering her. Maybe they *could* use the lunch sack. She and Juan wouldn't go far. She could keep an eye on the lunch while they gathered nuts.

Josefina covered the fire with ashes and moved the stew away from the heat. Then she helped Juan untie the lunch sack and empty it. She folded a corner of the blanket over the lunch. "Come on," she said. "We'll pick up the nuts that have fallen from the trees around here."

Juan happily took her hand. "We'll find the most nuts of anyone," he said, "and get the reward!"

Josefina looked at Juan's big brown eyes so full of hope. She didn't have the heart to tell him that they'd surely collect the *fewest* nuts of anyone. "We'll do our best," she said.

She and Juan did try hard. Juan scurried from tree to tree and pounced on every nut, crying, "Here's one!" But there weren't very many piñon trees near the clearing. Even after they'd gathered every single nut under every single tree, their sack was still pitifully light.

"This isn't enough!" Juan said, holding up the nearly empty bag. "We need more."

Josefina felt sorry for him. "I have an idea!" she said. "I'll shake the trunks of the trees to make the nuts fall down. I've seen Papá do it." Josefina wrapped her arms around the trunk of the nearest piñon tree and shook it as hard as she could. But only a few handfuls of nuts fell. Juan collected them and dropped them into the bag. They made no difference at all.

Juan sighed. "The tree is too big," he said, "and you are too small."

"Sí," agreed Josefina. Juan was right. Her skinny arms and legs were more the size of the branches of the tree than the sturdy trunk. She gazed up into the branches waving gracefully above her head, and all at once she had another idea.

"I'll climb up and bounce on the branches," she said to Juan. "That'll make the nuts fall!"

Josefina clambered up the tree. For the first time that day, she was *glad* she was so small. None of her sisters would have fitted between the prickly, pokey, needly branches of the tree as she did.

Josefina stood on a branch, held on to the trunk of the tree, bent her knees, and bounced. The branch dipped and swayed under her weight, and the piñón nuts fell like rain all around Juan.

Juan crowed with delight as he collected the nuts. "Do it again, Josefina!" he cried. "Bounce some more!"

Josefina did. And after she had bounced on every possible branch on *that* tree, she and Juan moved on to another tree, and another, and another, each tree a little bit farther away from the clearing. With every bounce on every branch, nuts showered down, pelting Juan and plopping to the ground. Juan cheerfully put them in his sack, which grew fatter and fatter.

Josefina was scratched and her hair was full of twigs, but she didn't care. As she bounced on the highest branch of the tallest piñón tree of all, she looked back toward the clearing. Something moving near the campfire caught her eye.

Oh no! There was a squirrel, bold as could be, nibbling at the lunch! "Shoo! Shoo! Shoo!" Josefina shouted at the squirrel as she frantically scrambled down the tree. "Quick, Juan! Run back! There's a squirrel eating the lunch!"

Juan hurried, but his fat little legs couldn't carry him very fast. The squirrel wasn't the least bit afraid. With its tiny front paws it took something that was

small and brown from the lunch and
popped it into its mouth before
it skittered away. By the time
Josefina was on the ground, the
squirrel was up a tall cottonwood tree.
Josefina saw the tip of its feathery tail
disappearing into a hole in the tree's
trunk.

Juan and Josefina stood at the
bottom of the tree staring up. "You bad
squirrel!" yelled Juan. "You stealer! Come
back!"

As if it understood, the squirrel came
out of its hole. This time it had a piñón
nut in its paws.

"Where did you get that nut?"
Josefina asked the squirrel. "Not from

our lunch. And your hole is not in a piñón tree."

The squirrel looked at Josefina with its bright, mischievous eyes. Then it scampered farther up the tree and balanced on a branch, chattering and scolding.

Suddenly, Josefina felt excited. "That squirrel is trying to distract us," she said, "and I bet I know why. Quick, Juan! Get the sack."

The cottonwood tree did not have low branches, so Josefina had to hug the trunk and shinny up to the branch just below the squirrel's hole. She reached into the hole and then whooped for joy. "Juan!" she shouted. "The hole is full of nuts! Hundreds and hundreds of nuts!"

"Hurray!" shouted Juan. Josefina tossed down handful after handful of nuts. Juan stood below, holding out his arms and smiling as nuts fell all around him. *Plip, plop, plippetty, ploppetty, plip!*

"Josefina!" exclaimed Tía Dolores. "You and Juan have done a lovely job of setting out the lunch for us. Gracias."

Josefina beamed. She and Juan had spread the lunch out on the blanket, so that it was ready and waiting when everyone returned to the clearing. There was soft, white goat cheese, ripe plums, small sweet apples, spicy chile stew, and

Josefina tossed down handful after handful of nuts.

cold meat. There were *tortillas* and big, round *buñuelos* in the bread basket.

tortillas and buñuelos

Francisca sank to her knees on the blanket and sighed dramatically. "I'm sure I collected the most nuts," she said. "My sack's so heavy it made me tired to carry it."

"Mine's heavier!" said Clara.

"No, it isn't," said Francisca.

"Yes, it is!" said Clara.

Papá held up his hand to stop them. "Let's see, shall we?" he said.

Francisca, Clara, Ana, Tía Dolores, and Papá put their sacks all in a line. "Well," said Papá after he had lifted each one. "All the sacks are quite heavy.

You've all done a fine job, but I think the heaviest sack belongs to—"

"Excuse me, Papá," Josefina interrupted. "Juan and I collected nuts, too. We'd like to ask you to lift our sack."

Josefina heard Francisca whisper to Clara, "Poor Josefina! There's not a way in the world she and Juan could have collected as many nuts as either one of *us*!"

"Where is your sack?" asked Papá.

Juan and Josefina grinned at each other. "There it is!" cried Juan, pointing. "Under the big tree!"

Everyone looked and gasped. The sack was bulging! It was much fatter than any of the other sacks. Juan and Josefina's sack was filled to the top, almost *overflowing* with nuts!

Papá laughed out loud. He walked over to the tree, grasped the sack in two hands, and pretended to struggle to lift it. "Bless my soul!" he said. "This sack is the heaviest by far. It's easy to see who collected the most nuts this year!" He smiled at Josefina and Juan. "Well done, little ones," he said. "You deserve the reward." Papá came back to the blanket and looked through the lunch. Then he looked again, and again. At last he said, "I'm sorry, children. I can't find the reward. It was a *piloncillo*, a little cone of hard brown sugar. I wonder what happened to it."

Juan and Josefina grinned at each other again. "A squirrel stole it!" said Juan.

"That's too bad!" said Papá.

"Sí," said Josefina. "But it's only fair. You see, Juan and I stole the squirrel's piñón nuts. I climbed up the tree and found them in his hole."

"María Josefina Montoya!" exclaimed Tía Dolores. "I thought you were an extraordinary girl the first moment I met you, and now I'm sure of it! How clever of you—and you, too, Juan." Tía Dolores hugged Juan, and then she hugged Josefina. As she did, she whispered in Josefina's ear, "I am proud of you."

Josefina hugged Tía Dolores back.

She was *glad* the squirrel had stolen the reward of brown sugar. For her, no reward on earth could be sweeter than Tía Dolores's praise.

VALERIE TRIPP

At 9   *Now*

One of my favorite books about New Mexico is called *The Good Life*. It was written in 1949 by a New Mexican woman with the beautiful name of Fabiola Cabeza de Baca Gilbert. She describes a family going to the foothills of the mountains to gather piñón nuts and having a picnic just as Josefina's family does in this story.

Valerie Tripp has written twenty-one books in The American Girls Collection, including six about Josefina.

Looking
back
1824

A PEEK INTO
THE PAST

Rancho Life in 1824

The Montoyas gathered piñón nuts during the autumn harvest, but there was work to do on the rancho all year

The rancho provided everything the family needed to survive.

round. Men and boys worked in the fields and tended animals, and girls and women cooked, gardened, and tended the home. Families built their ranchos near rivers and streams. In the dry land of New Mexico, water was their most important resource.

Streams brought melting snow from the mountains to the dry land. Farmers planted their crops near a stream and dug networks of *acequias*, or irrigation ditches, to carry water from the stream to their crops.

Several families shared one main acequia. A *mayordomo*, or elected official, was in charge of it. He decided how much water each rancho was allowed

The main acequia in Albuquerque in the 1880s

and when the rancho was scheduled to receive water.

In the spring, the acequias had to be

cleaned. All of the families who lived on the acequia worked together to clear it of mud, grass, and stones.

Each family cleared the acequias that flowed into their own fields.

By late spring, the acequias were clean and overflowing with water. Now the growing season could begin.

Farmers planted crops that were originally from Spain, such as wheat, carrots, and apricots. They also planted native foods like squash, beans, and corn.

Each spring, the women and children gave their homes and churches a fresh coat of *adobe*, or mud plaster. Children loved to spread the plaster on the walls with their bare hands and smooth the plaster on the roof with their bare feet!

Girls and women also planted a kitchen garden in the spring. They grew fresh vegetables, fruits, and herbs that they used every day.

Girls plastering the walls of their rancho

Through the summer, families tended and watered their gardens and crops. The women and girls carried water in large pottery jars, called *tinajas*, from the stream to the gardens. The families had to make sure they had healthy, plentiful crops so the food would last through the winter.

tinaja

When fall came, it was time to harvest the gardens and fields. The men brought in the crops from the fields. The girls and women gathered crops from the gardens and orchards and preserved food for the winter.

Drying corn and chiles

Corn was an important harvest crop. Girls and women ground dried kernels into flour for tortillas. They also roasted ears of corn in an *horno*. Roasted corn was eaten as a sweet snack, called *chicos*, or soaked in lime and boiled for a stew called *posole*.

*This woman is roasting corn in an **horno**, or outdoor oven.*

The girls and women also preserved fruits, vegetables, and herbs from the kitchen garden. They strung chile *ristras* and slices of squash to dry, they buried melons in sand to keep them fresh, and they hung herbs to dry in bunches near the kitchen hearth.

Meat was also preserved in the fall. Animals from the family's herds of goats, sheep, and cattle were butchered. Then the meat was cut into thin strips and dried in the open air.

*Meat was dried in thin strips, called **jerky**.*

While they worked, they had fun sharing gossip and news, telling stories, and singing songs. The harvest was hard work, but it was important to make sure everyone had enough food for the winter. If a family had a bad harvest, neighbors made sure they didn't go hungry.

Toward the end of the harvest, it was time to gather piñón nuts. Piñón trees provided wood for fires and nuts for food. Piñón nuts were also a valuable trade item. A good crop of piñón nuts came only every few years, so it was cause for celebration. The fastest way to gather the nuts that were still on the tree was to shake the tree until the nuts fell like rain! Once all the nuts were gathered, families could look forward to winter evenings roasting and eating the sweet nuts before the fire.

Piñón nuts were ripe when the cones fell from the trees.

An
American
Girls
Pastime

MAKE A PASTEL
*Piñón nuts make this New Mexican
pastry delicious.*

At harvest time, Josefina and her
family walked into the foothills of the
mountains to gather piñón nuts. Most of
the nuts were used to trade for things the
family needed. But they tasted too good
to give them all away! On winter
evenings, Francisca and Josefina loved to
sit by the fire and roast the nuts so they
could eat them one after another. You can
enjoy the delicious taste of the piñón nut
by making this *pastel*.

YOU WILL NEED:

 An adult to help you

Ingredients

For the pastry:

2 cups flour

$1/2$ teaspoon baking powder

1 teaspoon salt

$2/3$ cup lard

6 to 9 tablespoons cold water

For the filling:

1 16-ounce can of pumpkin

$1/2$ cup raisins, chopped

$1/2$ cup pine nuts, chopped

$1/2$ cup sugar

$1/2$ teaspoon allspice

$1/2$ teaspoon cinnamon

$1/4$ teaspoon nutmeg

For the topping:

2 tablespoons melted butter

1 tablespoon sugar

$1/2$ teaspoon cinnamon

Equipment

2 large mixing bowls

Measuring cups and spoons

2 wooden spoons

Pastry cutter or fork

Clean towel

Rolling pin

Pie pan

Small cookie cutters

Knife

Pastry brush

Small bowl

Potholders

1. Preheat the oven to 350°. Combine the flour, baking powder, and salt in a mixing bowl.

2. Add the lard. Use the pastry cutter or fork to work it into the mixture.

3. Add the cold water until a dough is formed. Have an adult help you knead the dough. Cover the dough with the towel and set it aside for $1/2$ hour.

4. Prepare the filling. In a separate mixing bowl, combine the pumpkin, raisins, pine nuts, sugar, allspice, cinnamon, and nutmeg. Mix well.

5. Divide the dough in half. Flour the counter and roll out half of the dough. Roll it into a circle large enough to fit the pie pan.

6. Place the dough in the pie pan. Make sure the edges of the dough go up the sides of the pan. Spread the filling over the dough.

7. Roll out the second half of the dough. If you like, use cookie cutters to make designs on the top.

8. Place the top over the filling. Pinch the edges together to form a seal. Cut several slits in the top of the pastry to let the steam escape.

9. Use the pastry brush to brush the melted butter on the top pastry. In the small bowl, mix the sugar and cinnamon together. Sprinkle it over the top.

10. Bake for about an hour, or until the pastry is brown and the filling is bubbling. Remove it from the oven and let it cool slightly before serving.

Glossary of Spanish Words

acequia *(ah-SEH-kee-ah)*—a ditch made to carry water to a farmer's fields

adobe *(ah-DOH-beh)*—a building material made of earth mixed with straw and water

buñuelo *(boo-nyoo-EH-lo)*—fried bread served with a glaze or sugar and cinnamon

chicos *(CHEE-kohs)*—corn on the cob that has been roasted, steamed, and dried

gracias *(GRAH-see-ahs)*—thank you

horno *(OR-no)*—an outdoor oven made of adobe

mayordomo *(mah-yor-DOH-mo)*—a man who is elected to take charge of the acequia

pastel *(pah-STEL)*—a pastry filled with fruit

piloncillo *(pee-lohn-SEE-yo)*—a small sugar cone

piñón *(pee-NYOHN)*—a kind of short, scrubby pine that produces delicious nuts

posole *(po-SO-leh)*—a stew made of preserved corn

rancho *(RAHN-cho)*—a farm or ranch where crops are grown and animals are raised

rebozo *(reh-BO-so)*—a long shawl worn by girls and women

ristra *(REE-strah)*—a string of chiles

sí *(SEE)*—yes

tía *(TEE-ah)*—aunt

tinaja *(tee-NAH-hah)*—a large pottery jar used to carry water

tortillas *(tor-TEE-yahs)*—a kind of flat, round bread made of corn or wheat

THE AMERICAN GIRLS COLLECTION®

To learn more about The American Girls Collection, fill out the postcard below and mail it to American Girl, or call **1-800-845-0005**. We'll send you a free catalogue full of books, dolls, dresses, and other delights for girls.

I'm an American girl who loves to get mail. Please send me a catalogue of The American Girls Collection:

My name is _____

My address is _____

City _____ State _____ Zip _____

My birth date is ___ / ___ / ___
                Month   Day   Year   1961

And send a catalogue to my friend:

My friend's name is _____

Address _____

City _____ State _____ Zip _____
                                                1225